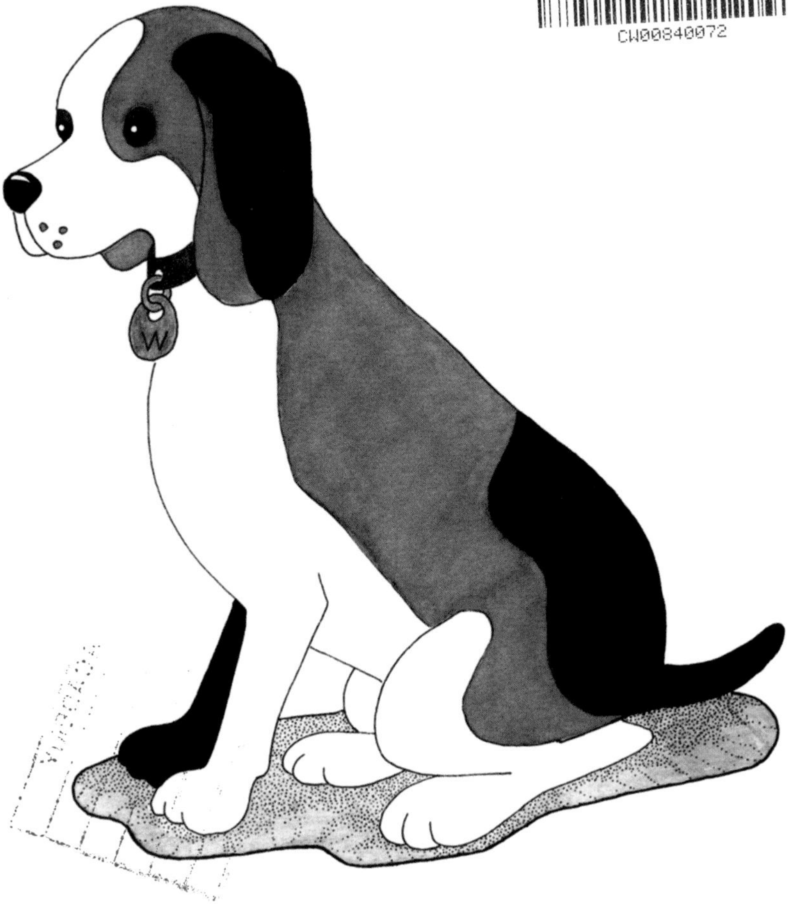

a dog

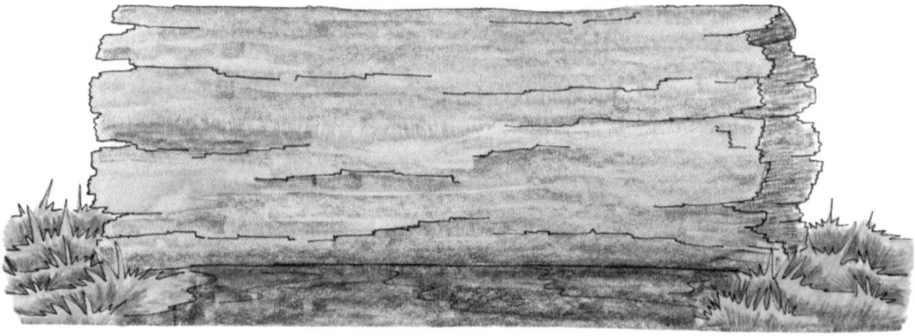

a log

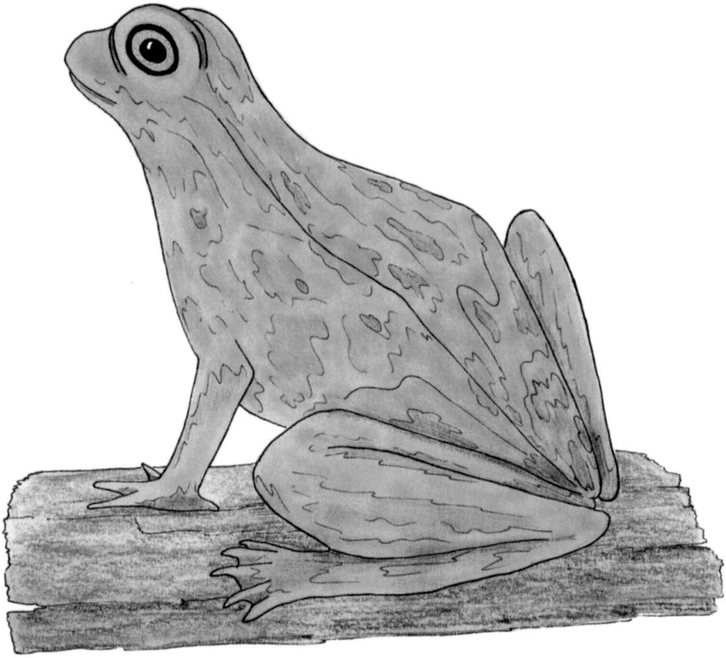

a frog

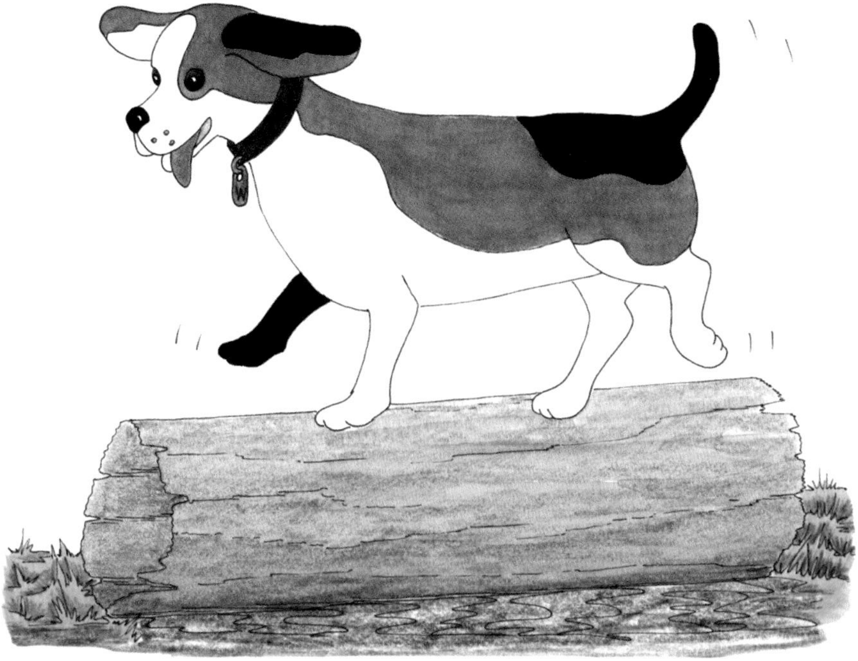

a dog on a log

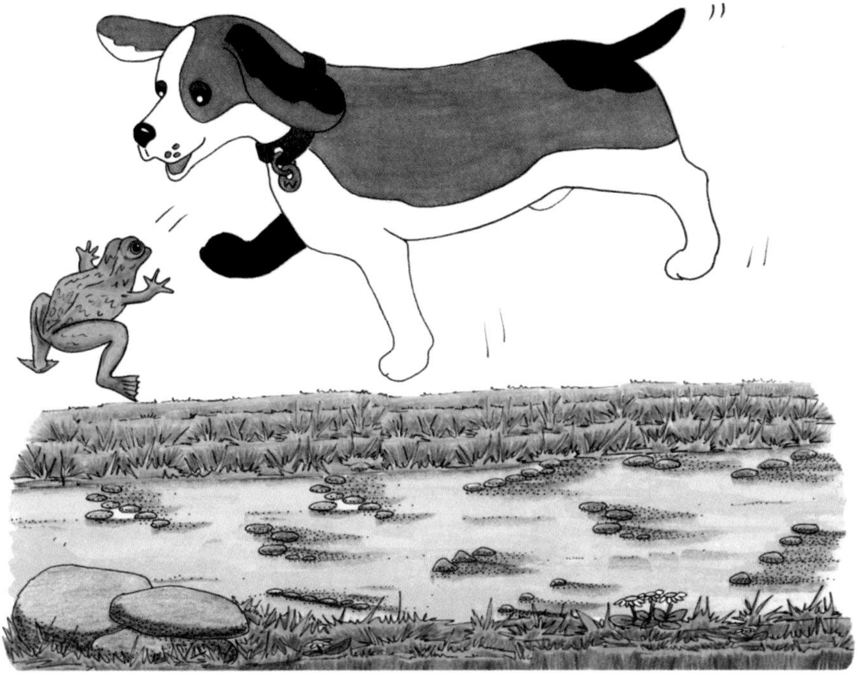

a dog and
a frog

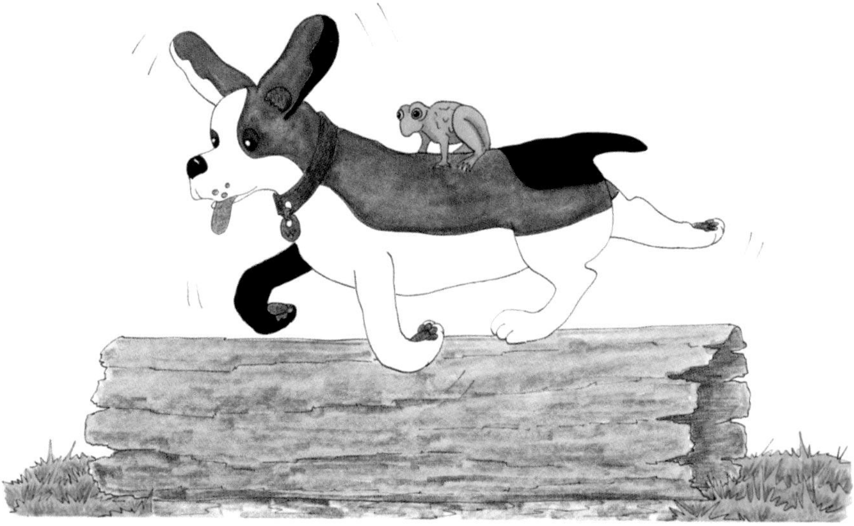

a frog and
a dog on a log

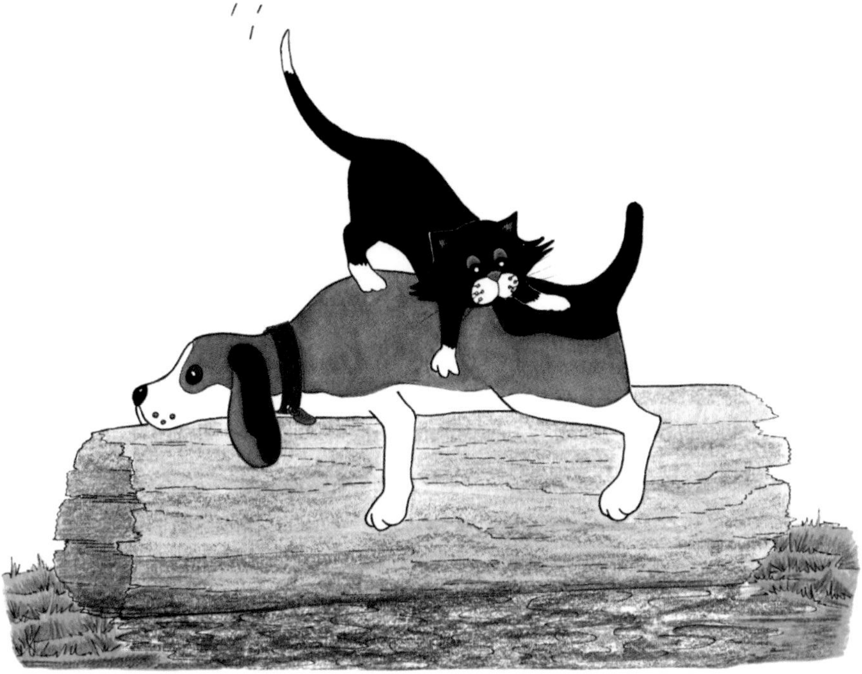

a cat and
a dog on a log

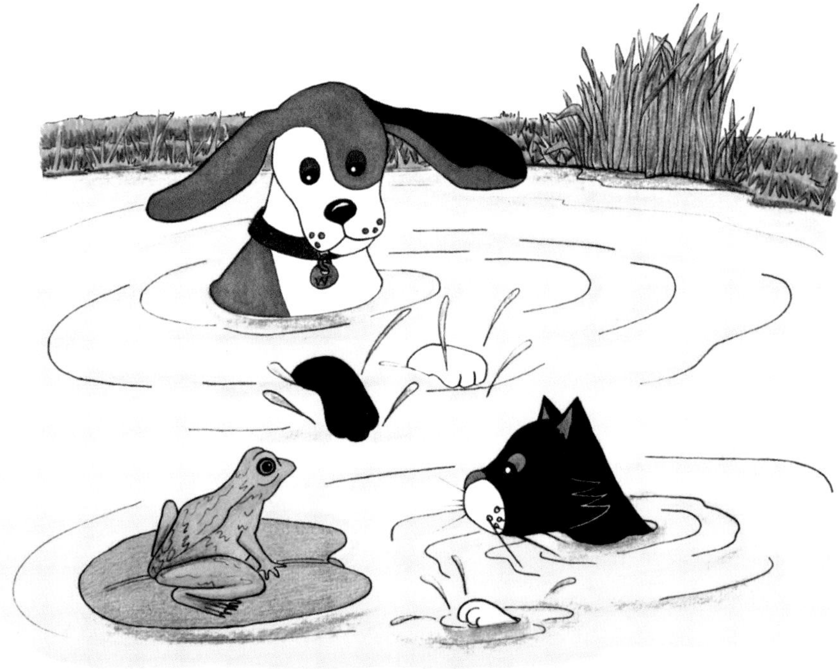

a cat and a dog

and a frog